W9-COT-211

AUTOMOBILE MECHANICS ON THE JOB

BY LAURA LANE

MOMENTUM

Published by The Child's World®
1980 Lookout Drive • Mankato, MN 56003-1705
800-599-READ • www.childsworld.com

Content Consultant: Mitchell D. Connor, ASE Certified Master Technician, Automotive Instructor, Lake Superior College

Photographs ©: Shutterstock Images, cover, 1, 12, 16, 20, 22, 23; iStockphoto, 5, 10, 18; Hodag Media/Shutterstock Images, 6, 8, 11; Sergei Bachlakov/Shutterstock Images, 9; Dean Mitchell/iStockphoto, 14; Avalon Studio/iStockphoto, 17; Pavel L Photo and Video/Shutterstock Images, 24; Michael Jung/Shutterstock Images, 27; Rob Wilson/Shutterstock Images, 28

ISBN 9781503835566
LCCN 2019942958

Printed in the United States of America

CONTENTS

FAST FACTS

What's the Job?

- Automobile mechanics inspect, **diagnose**, and repair problems in cars. They also do basic **maintenance** on cars, such as oil changes.
- Taking high school classes in car repair, electronics, computers, small engines, and mathematics is a good place to begin training as an automobile mechanic.
- People who want to do this job after high school can go into an automotive service technology program. The program can last one to two years. Mechanics can also start out as **apprentices** and learn on the job from more experienced mechanics.

Important Stats

- In 2018, there were approximately 648,050 automobile mechanics in the United States.
- By 2026, the number of jobs for automobile mechanics is expected to increase by 6 percent.
- In 2018, automobile mechanics made around $43,730 per year.

People expect automobile mechanics ► to be able to fix their vehicles.

HITACH
HITACH
MIDAS
MUTUAL
OMAHA
25
FUZZY
FUZZY'S
20

CHAPTER ONE

RACING TO GET THE JOB DONE

Hundreds of thousands of fans cheered as brightly colored cars raced past them. The cars were on a long oval track known as the Indianapolis Motor Speedway in Indiana. The drivers were competing in the Indianapolis 500, one of the fastest and most dangerous car races in the world.

Drivers went around the track at speeds of more than 220 miles per hour (354 km/h). A shiny green car broke from the pack and pulled into the **pit**. A crew of six mechanics waited for it. They wore fire suits, fire-resistant footwear and gloves, and helmets. As soon as the car stopped, the mechanics sprang into action. They lifted the car off the ground using an air jack, and they connected the fuel hose to the car. They removed the car's tires and put on new ones. Then, they dropped the car back to the ground.

◄ **Indy cars are some of the fastest types of race cars.**

▲ During pit stops, mechanics make sure the car is working properly.

The chief mechanic signaled to the driver. The signal meant the driver could leave. The driver exited the pit and raced back onto the track. The entire pit stop took less than ten seconds. The mechanics worked quickly and accurately. Mistakes could make the difference between the driver winning or losing the race.

▲ **Mechanics will sometimes work together to figure out issues with cars.**

Race car drivers enjoy the spotlight, but the mechanics play a very important role in the sport as well.

Like athletes, pit crew mechanics must be strong. Many of them work with athletic trainers in order to stay in excellent shape and avoid getting injured. In 2009, Anna Chatten became the first female mechanic to be a member of an elite six-person pit crew. During one pit stop, Chatten lifted a 35-pound (15.8-kg) wheel with one hand during a tire change. Another time, she broke her foot during a pit stop. Chatten's job was dangerous. She had to fully concentrate and stay calm under pressure.

▲ **Race car tires can wear out fast on the race track.**

Chatten got her first taste of racing as a child. Growing up in Illinois, she raced go-carts. Over the years, she learned how to make repairs on her go-cart. When Chatten was 18 years old, she decided to become a race car mechanic. She attended a school for race mechanics in California. After graduating from school, she landed a job. She worked hard and was successful. Being a woman in the car racing world hasn't always been easy. One time a fan told her that she should let a man do her job instead. But Chatten's success proves that mechanics can be a person of any gender.

The pit stop crew needs to be quick if they want their racer to do well. ►

verizon
HITACHI
TEAM PENSKE
MECHANIX WEAR

ENGINE
SEE OWNER'S MANUAL

CHAPTER TWO

LEARNING THE ROPES

Sixteen-year-old Tim stared at the different parts of the old Volkswagen car engine in front of him. He was trying to figure out how to put the engine together. Tim liked working with his hands and building things. He also enjoyed solving problems. Putting the engine together was like solving a very difficult puzzle.

Rebuilding the engine wasn't easy. Tim read a manual about Volkswagen cars. He talked with auto mechanics at the repair shop near his home. He tried many different ways of putting the engine back together. Finally, he put the parts back together in the correct way.

Tim knew that the things he liked to do were the same as what auto mechanics did on the job. Mechanics work with car parts and tools. They need good hand-eye coordination and steady hands. They must pay attention to small details.

◄ Car engines can look complicated to people who aren't familiar with them.

▲ **It's important that automobile mechanics wear the right equipment when working on cars.**

Mechanics also use computers to look up information and help diagnose problems in cars. And they need to explain to customers what is wrong with their cars. Being friendly and a good listener are important qualities for an automobile mechanic.

Tim made a big decision. He wanted to become an auto mechanic. He signed up for a class on automotive repair at his high school. In the class, he learned about the different systems of a car and how they all work together. He also landed a job as an apprentice at a large auto repair shop near his house.

The mechanics all wore the same uniform: a light blue shirt, navy pants, and work boots. Tim wore this uniform, too.

The front of the auto repair shop was cozy and comfortable, with couches, chairs, and a television. Customers could wait and relax there while their cars were getting fixed. The back of the shop was the garage area. That was where the mechanics repaired cars. Often there were several cars lifted high into the air on **hoists**. Tim could walk under the cars without hitting his head. The garage area was very busy and sometimes noisy. Several mechanics worked on different cars at the same time. They talked back and forth to one another.

Tim started his apprenticeship by watching how an experienced mechanic performed basic maintenance on a car. The mechanic changed the car's oil and checked the car's fluid levels and tire pressure. As he watched, Tim asked the mechanic questions. Then, Tim popped open the car's hood and peered inside. He also looked underneath the car. He thought one of the car parts looked like a big, fat worm. The mechanic told him that the worm-shaped object was the exhaust. The exhaust was a pipe that carried gas out of the engine of the car. The exhaust contained a **catalytic converter**. It cleaned the gasses coming out of the car before they went into the air.

▲ **Oil is important for car engines to run properly.**

Tim worked hard. Soon, he was performing basic oil changes by himself. After he graduated from high school, Tim continued his work as an apprentice at the auto repair shop. He also went to an automotive technology program at a local community college. Eventually, he became a certified auto technician. He achieved this by passing tests through the National Institute for Automotive Service Excellence (ASE).

Today, car technology is changing rapidly. Auto mechanics must constantly learn new things in order to stay on top of their profession.

◄ **Hoists allow mechanics to easily work under cars.**

CHAPTER THREE

BREAKING THE GENDER BARRIER

Patrice Banks was filled with dread. She stared at the dashboard of her green car. A warning light had come on. The light meant her car might have a minor or more serious problem. She knew her car needed a mechanic. But she hated the idea of taking it into an auto repair shop. Banks wasn't very knowledgeable about cars or how they worked. She felt ignorant and uncomfortable when talking with a mechanic. She never took her car in for regular oil changes and tire checks. Now, she had no choice.

A mechanic inspected Banks's car. He said there was a problem with the **transmission**. It would cost $1,700 to repair it. Banks was angry and upset that the repair would cost so much. But she needed her car. She told the mechanic to fix the transmission. After the repair, Banks discovered a new problem.

◄ **Automobile mechanics are also called automotive service technicians, or service techs.**

▲ Car repairs can be expensive, depending on what's wrong with the car.

Her car began to shake when it was in the park or neutral gears. Banks took her car back into the repair shop. Then, months later, the warning light started flashing on her dash again.

Banks felt frustrated. She wished she knew more about cars. She wanted to figure out what was wrong with her car by herself. During college, Banks had studied engineering.

She loved math and science. After college, she worked as an engineer for a large chemical company. As a successful engineer, Banks found it difficult not to know how to fix her own car.

Banks talked with other women and discovered they felt the same way. Many of them wanted to know more about car care and repairs. Banks did an online search and found there were not many female mechanics in the United States.

Banks wanted to take her car to a female mechanic. She felt less intimidated and more comfortable talking with women about car repairs. She couldn't find a female auto mechanic near her, so she became one. Banks took night classes in an automotive technology program. She was the only woman in her class. At age 31, she was also the oldest student in the class, but she didn't care. Banks loved learning about cars. She always wanted to know exactly how the systems in the cars worked. Banks eventually quit her job as an engineer to work as a mechanic. While still in auto school, Banks worked at some mechanic shops. Then, she decided to open the Girls Auto Clinic shop in Philadelphia. It's a full-service auto repair shop.

Banks also began leading Girls Auto Clinic workshops. At the first workshop, about 20 female students drove their cars to a parking lot at the University of Delaware for the class.

▲ **People jump-start their cars when their car battery needs a charge.**

First, the students gathered around a table in the parking lot. The table was stacked with car parts, including brake lines, brake pads, spark plugs, and air filters. Like show-and-tell in school, Banks picked up each part and explained what it was and how it worked in a car. She let the students feel and examine all the parts.

Next, Banks showed the students how to pop their vehicle's hoods. She taught them how to jump-start their cars, change air filters, and measure tire pressure. The workshop was a success, and Banks has held more than 40 classes since then. She also began handing out small pamphlets at her workshops.

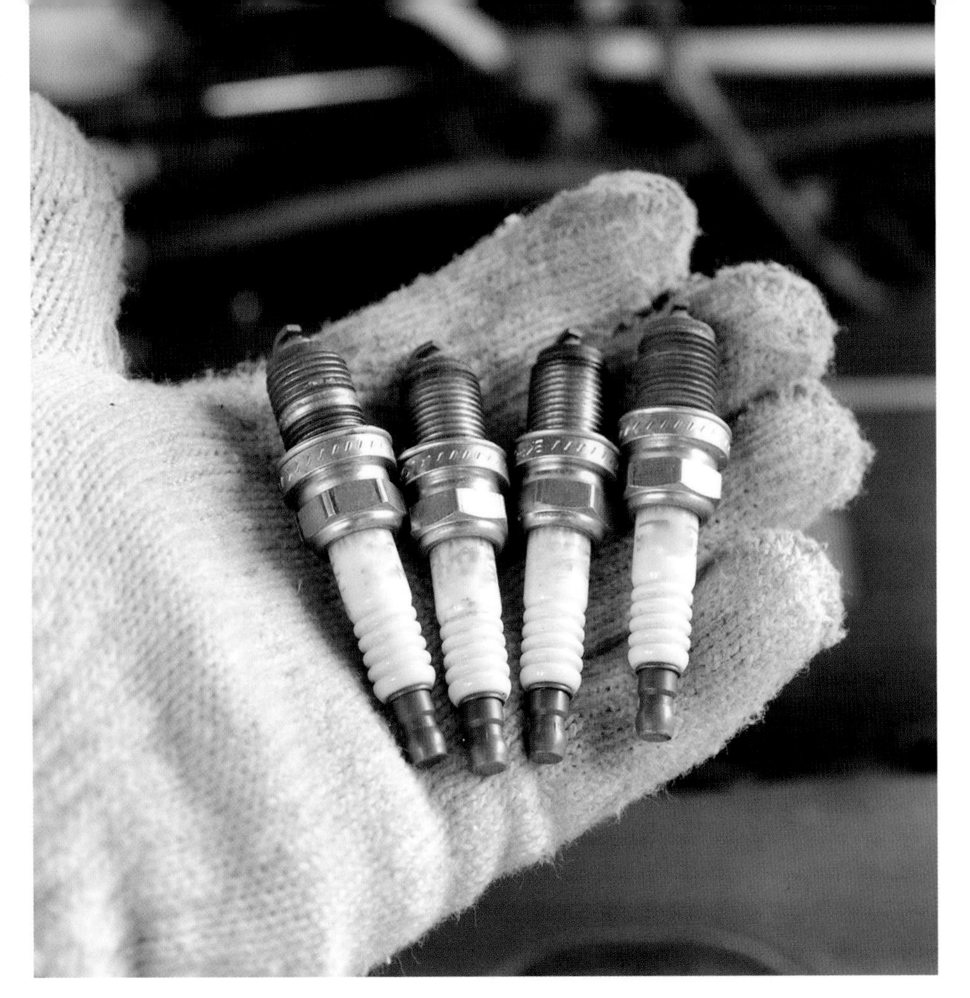

▲ Old spark plugs can cause issues such as lower gas mileage.

The purpose of the pamphlets was to educate women about the basics of car maintenance and repairs. This pamphlet grew into Banks's first book, *Girls Auto Clinic Glove Box Guide*. Banks wants to help women feel knowledgeable about how to take care of their cars. She also wants to encourage more women to become auto mechanics.

CHAPTER FOUR

LIFE ON THE JOB

The auto repair shop was filled with sounds. Mechanics shouted back and forth to one another happily as they worked on cars. Justin, an experienced mechanic, stood in the front of the shop at the service counter. He leaned forward so he could hear what his customer, Lisa, was saying. Lisa spoke very quickly. She was worried about her car. She told Justin that a bright yellow light was flashing on her dashboard. The yellow light was a signal to check the car's computer network system. Lisa knew something was wrong with her car. She needed a mechanic to figure out the problem and fix it.

Justin listened carefully as Lisa described the problem. He asked Lisa several questions. Was the car running differently than it normally did? Lisa said yes. Did it take longer to start the car? Yes. Did the car act funny when she stepped on the gas? Yes.

◄ Auto shops can only handle a certain number of cars at once.

Lisa said the car felt slower than normal when she was trying to go faster. Justin asked Lisa to leave the car with him. He wanted to run tests on it. He gave Lisa an idea of how long it would take to run the tests and how much it might cost.

Once Lisa agreed, Justin got to work. He plugged a tool called a scanner into a port underneath the car's dashboard. Once it was plugged in, the scanner analyzed the car's computer system. A code popped up on the scanner's screen. The code was a letter with three numbers. The code meant Lisa's car was not getting the correct amount of fuel when it was running.

After using the scanner, Justin looked under the car's hood and did a visual inspection. There were many rubber hoses under the hood called vacuum lines. The vacuum lines control many different things, such as the car's braking system. Justin looked for any cracks or holes in the vacuum lines. He noticed that one of the lines was loose. Justin thought this was the source of the problem. He reattached the vacuum line. Then he ran the scanner again. The scanner readings on Lisa's car were normal. Justin called Lisa and told her the good news. He let her know the cost of the repair was the same as his original estimate.

Good customer service is one important ► part of being an automobile mechanic.

▲ **A Toyota Prius is one type of hybrid vehicle.**

Before Lisa picked up her car, Justin did one more thing. He took the car for a test drive. Lisa's car was running smoothly again. Lisa was relieved and grateful to Justin for fixing her car.

After Lisa paid for the repair and left, Justin turned his attention to his next customer, Mike, who owned a hybrid car.

Hybrid cars have both a small gasoline engine and an electrical engine. Mike bought the hybrid car because it runs primarily on electricity, not **fossil fuels**. His hybrid car is better for the environment. That's because it does not pollute the air as much as a regular car does.

Justin attended frequent trainings in order to stay up to date on how to repair electrical cars. Some mechanics told Justin that they were worried about keeping on top of the quick changes in car technology. But Justin was up to the challenge. He was excited to learn new things and was glad he had chosen to become an auto mechanic.

THINK ABOUT IT

- Why are mechanics important in everyday life?
- How do you think the job of an automobile mechanic might change in the future?
- What types of skills do mechanics need when they work with customers?

GLOSSARY

apprentices (uh-PREN-tis-ses): Apprentices learn on the job from a more experienced worker. The apprentices watched the mechanic work on the car engine.

catalytic converter (kat-uh-LIT-ik kun-VUR-tur): A catalytic converter is a part inside a car that cleans gasses from the car as they are released into the air. The catalytic converter reduces air pollution because it cleans gasses coming out of a car.

diagnose (dye-uhg-NOHS): To diagnose something means to find signs that show the source of a problem. The auto mechanic had to diagnose what was wrong with the engine.

fossil fuels (FAH-suhl FYOO-uhlz): Fossil fuels are either oil, coal, or natural gas that are formed from the remains of ancient animals and plants. Many cars need fossil fuels to work.

hoists (HOYSTS): Hoists are tools that mechanics use to lift cars off the ground and into the air. In the auto repair shop, cars were on hoists so the mechanics could look underneath them.

maintenance (MAY-tuh-nuhns): Maintenance means to perform tasks to take care of equipment or property. Cars require basic maintenance such as oil changes and tire rotations.

pit (PIT): A pit is an area near a racecourse where cars can be fixed and refueled. The race car driver pulled into the pit.

transmission (trans-MISH-uhn): A transmission is a group of parts in a car, including speed changing gears, that transfers power from the engine to wheels. The transmission wasn't working properly in the vehicle.

BOOKS

Eason, Sarah. *How Does a Car Work?* New York, NY: Gareth Stevens Publishing, 2010.

Gregory, Josh. *Henry Ford: Father of the Auto Industry.* New York, NY: Children's Press, 2014.

Monnig, Alex. *Behind the Wheel of an Indy Car.* Mankato, MN: The Child's World, 2016.

WEBSITES

Visit our website for links about automobile mechanics: **childsworld.com/links**

Note to Parents, Teachers, and Librarians: We routinely verify our Web links to make sure they are safe and active sites. So encourage your readers to check them out!

SELECTED BIBLIOGRAPHY

"Automotive Service Technicians and Mechanics." *Bureau of Labor Statistics*, 29 Mar. 2019, bls.gov. Accessed 2 May 2019.

Banks, Patrice. *Girls Auto Clinic Glove Box Guide*. New York, NY: Touchstone, 2017.

Fernandez, Megan. "Meet the Indianapolis 500's Top Female Mechanic." *Indianapolis Monthly*, 23 May 2015, indianapolismonthly.com. Accessed 2 May 2019.

INDEX

ABOUT THE AUTHOR

Laura Lane grew up in Denver, Colorado. She attended the University of Colorado and earned degrees in English and law. After her daughter and son were born, she decided to pursue her dream of writing books for children. She and her husband, children, dogs, and cats now live in Madison, Wisconsin.